CW00662936

First published in 2020by:
(Hazel P Marsay)

[ISBN: 978-1-3999-0233-5]

Printed and bound in Great Britain by:
Book Printing UK Remus House, Coltsfoot Drive, Woodston, Peterborough PE2 9BF

A DOLL IN A VELVET GOWN

A CHILD SITS IN THE POURING RAIN
HER CLOTHES ARE ALL IN RAGS
WHILE PEOPLE PASSING BY HER
JUST STAND AND LOOK, AND STARE.

HER HAIR HANGS DOWN IN RINGLETS
HER EYES SO BIG AND BROWN
AND IN HER HAND SHE CARRIES
A DOLL IN A VELVET GOWN.

BESIDE HER ON THE GROUND
IS A DOG AS WET AS SHE
PATTING HIS HEAD SHE WHISPERS
HERE DOG STAY WITH ME.

LOOK, THE RAINS STOPPED FALLING
NO CLOUDS UP IN THE SKY
THE GIRL GETS UP THEN WALKS AWAY
AND I TRY HARD NOT TO CRY.

A SONG OF LOVE

A RED RED ROSE
I GIVE TO YOU
TO PROVE MY LOVE
FOR YOU IS TRUE.

BRING ME A SONG
A SONG OF LOVE
BRING ME YOUR HEART
AND THE STARS ABOVE.

TELL ME AGAIN
THE WAY YOUFEEL
TELL ME YOUR LOVE
IS LOVE THAT ISREAL.

TAKE ALL MY DREAMS
AND WRAP THEM IN GOLD
TAKE ALL MY MEMORIES
TO HAVE AND TOHOLD.

LOVE ME FOREVER
THE WAY I LOVE YOU
THEN WE'll BE TOGETHER
OUR DREAMS WILL COME TRUE.

ANOTHER DAY

STANDING IN THE POURING RAIN
PEOPLE PASSING BY
CLOTHES BEDRAGGLED HANGING DOWN
MISERY EVERYWHERE.

LOOKING THROUGH TIRED GLAZED EYES
I WONDER WHAT HESEES
ANOTHER DAY TO GATHER IN
THE MONEY HE WILL NEED.

HE RATTLES THE TIN BESIDE HIM
SOME COINS DROP TO THE GROUND
HIS HANDS ARE GETTING COLDER
AND HE UTTERS NOT A SOUND.

WHAT HAPPENED TO HIS PLANS AND DREAMS
HOW DID HE GET SO LOW
THE HAND OF FATE CAME CRUELLY
AND DEALT HIM ANOTHER BLOW.

TOMORROW AND THE NEXT DAY
WILL ONLY BRING MORE PAIN
PEOPLE PASSING BY HIM
WHILE HE'S STANDING IN THE RAIN.

BANG WALLOP

BANG WALLOP WHOOPS A DAISY
THERE IT GOES ONCE MORE
THERE'S SOMEONE IN THE PANTRY
BANGING ON THE DOOR.

CUPS AND SAUCERS FLYING NOISES
EVERYWHERE
LOOK THERE'S SOMEONE COMING
HE'S HIDING OVER THERE.

BANG WALLOP WHOOPS A DAISY
THERE HE GOES AGAIN
NOW HE'S VANISHED COMPLETELY
HE'LL BE BACK BUT I DON'T KNOW WHEN.

DEEP DESPAIR

THERE'S ONLY ONE MORE MILE TO GO
THE SUN SHINES HIGH ABOVE
BUT I AM FILLED WITH DEEP DESPAIR
FOR I'VE LOST YOU MY LOVE.

THERE SEEMS NO END I'M WEARY
THE ROAD IS LONG AND BENDS
IF ONLY I COULD SEE YOU
MY MISERY WOULD END.

OH WHY IS FATE SO CRUEL
WHY MUST WE SUFFER PAIN
AM I TO LIVE FOREVER
IN THE SHADOW OF YOUR NAME.

SOMEDAY WHEN IT'S ALL OVER
WHEN ALL IN LIFE IS GONE
YOU'LL COME TO ME MY DARLING
BACK WHERE YOUBELONG.

FAR AWAY

FAR AWAY I HEAR YOU CALL
AS I SIT ALL ALONE
THE WAVES CARESS THE SANDY SHORE
THAT YOU AND I HAVE KNOWN.

SUMMERS GONE, NOW AUTUMN CREEPS
AND YOUR NO LONGER HERE
YOU'VE LEFT ME WITH JUST MEMORIES
A LAUGH A SMILE A TEAR.

LONELY THE HEART THAT'S LOVED AND LOST
SILENT THE TEARS THAT FALL
LOST IN A WORLD OF MAKE BELIEVE
WILL YOU EVER COME BACK TO CALL.

SO LITTLE TIME WE HAD TO SHARE
WERE YOU EVER IN LOVE WITH ME
OH WHY DID YOU HAVE TO LEAVE ME
AND GO SAILING ACROSS THE SEA.

HIDING IN THE LAVENDER

HIDING IN THE LAVENDER
ONE BRIGHT AND SUNNY DAY
I SPIED A LITTLE BUTTERFLY
SO HAPPY IN HERPLAY

HER WINGS WERE LIKE SOFT VELVET
THEY HAD A GOLDEN SHEEN
IT REALLY WAS THE PRETTIEST
BUTTERFLY I HAD EVER SEEN.

SHE FLUTTERED IN AND OUT THE FLOWERS
NOT A CARE HAD SHE
I SAT AND WATCHED HER QUIETLY
AND WONDERED COULD SHE SEE ME.

A DRAGONFLY FLEW AROUND ME
AND SETTLED ON MY ARM
THE BUTTERFLY TOOK NO NOTICE
JUST KEEPING OUT OF HARM.

THE WORLD IS FULL OF WONDERS
SUCH BEAUTY TO THE EYES.
LITTLE CREATURES LIVING
BENEATH GODS BLUE BLUE SKY.

IF EVER YOU SHOULD PASS THIS WAY
TAKE A LITTLE PEEK
MAYBE ALL THE BUTTERFLIES
WILL BE PLAYING HIDE AND SEEK.

IN HEAVEN

I HELD YOUR HAND WHEN THREE
I HELD YOUR HAND WHENSEVEN
I HELD YOUR HAND WHEN TWENTY ONE
I'LL HOLD YOUR HAND IN HEAVEN.

THERE'S A LITTLE COTTAGE STANDS
BESIDE A SHADY TREE
THERE'S A LITTLE LADY WAITING THERE
WITH SANDWICHES AND TEA.

HAVE PITY ON ME SIR SHE SAID
FOR I AM COLD ANDWEAK
I HAVE TRAVELLED FAR TODAY
MY LIFE IS PRETTYBLEAK.

IS THAT A TEARDROP IN YOUR EYE

A THOUSAND YEARS AGO IT SEEMS
SINCE YOU AND I WERE YOUNG
AMONGST THE DAISY'S WE WOULD RUN
OUT PLAYING IN THE SUN.

LAUGHING, DANCING, MERRILY
NO CARES HAD YOU OR I
THE WORLD WAS OH SO MAGICAL
IS THAT A TEARDROP IN YOUREYE.

FOR WE WERE LIKE TWO BUTTERFLIES
FLUTTERING IN THE BREEZE
FLITTING HERE AND FLITTING THERE
HOW HAPPY YOU AND ME.

NOW MY EYES ARE DIMMER
BUT YOU I STILL CAN SEE
SITTING CLOSE BESIDE ME
WHERE YOU WILL ALWAYS BE.

LIFE LIFE LIFE

RED AND GOLD BRIGHTLY SHINING
YELLOW EVER BRIGHT AS THE SUN
BLUE AND SILVER UP ABOVE US
MELLOW GREENS WHEN DAY IS DONE.

FLYING IN THE SKY ABOVE
BIRDS WITH SPECKLED WINGS
BUTTERFLIES FLUTTERING GAILY
DANCING FLOWERS AND THINGS.

MOONLIGHT SHINING ON THE WATER
TREES SO TALL AND STRONG
MANY WORDS LEFT UNSPOKEN
THINGS GONE ON TOO LONG.

LIFE'S A PICTURE DECKED WITH FLOWERS
DREAMS OF PALACES AND KINGS
HAPPY HOURS SPENT IN LAUGHTER
LISTEN TO THAT BIRD THAT SINGS.

PITTER PATTER, RAIN IS FALLING
SOMEONES CRYING UP ABOVE
POOLS OF TEARS UPON YOUR PILLOW
SADNESS JOY AND LOVE.

LITTLE ANGEL

LITTLE ANGEL OF THE NIGHT
LET YOUR WINGS TAKE FLIGHT
SOARING UPWARDS TO THE STARS
WHAT A HEAVENLY SIGHT.

HIGHER NOW GO FLOATING
MOONBEAMS ALL AROUND
LITTLE CHILD OF PARADISE
MAKING NOT A SOUND.

A CHOIR OF SINGING ANGELS
KEEPING YOU FREE FROM HARM
WATCHING TENDERLY OVER YOU
ALL AROUND IS CALM.

LITTLE ANGEL OF THE NIGHT
I SEE YOU IN MYDREAMS
FLOATING BY ON CLOUDS OF WHITE
WITH SHINING SILVER BEAMS.

LOOK AMONGST THE HEATHER

THE HEATHER WAS SO PURPLE
AS I WALKED ACROSS THEMOORS
THE HAUNTINGS OF A BYGONE AGE
OF THIS I AM SO SURE.

A WIND WAS SOFTLY BLOWING
IT SEEMED TO SAY TO ME
LOOK AMONGST THE HEATHER
TELL ME WHAT YOUSEE.

A GREAT EXPANSE OF NO MAN'S LAND
COLD AND BLEAK I SEE
THE SMELL OF MOSS PEAT AND STRAW
LINGER NEXT TO ME.

SO LONELY YET SO BEAUTIFUL
A WONDROUS SIGHT TO SEE
THE HEATHER IS SO PURPLE
AND IT'S CALLING OUT TO ME.

MR MODEM

MR MODEMS GOT A RASH UPON HIS FACE
WE THINK HE'S GOT A VIRUS
FROM SOMEWHERE OUT OF SPACE
MR HARD DISK IS RUNNING UP AND DOWN
CHECKING OUT HIS SYSTEM, TO SEE WHY HE IS DOWN.

THERE'S BEEN SOME FUNNY THINGS HAPPENING ROUND HERE
IT ALWAYS SEEMS TO HAPPEN, WHEN MR VIRUS IS NEAR
THEY'VE EVEN CALLED THE DISC DOCTOR
HE DOESN'T KNOW WHAT TO DO
THEY'LL HAVE TO FETCH THE CID IN
TO SEE WHAT THEY CAN DO.

MR RAM THE MEMORY MAN SEEMS TO KNOW THE ANSWER
HE'S WORKING HARD AND WORKING LONG
TO TRY AND FIND THE CANCER
EMAILS COMING UP THE PATH HIS BAG IS OVERFLOWING
HE'S GOT TO SEE THE CID FOR THEY ARE IN THE KNOWING.

MR BRAIN THE CPU MAN SAYS I'VE SEEN THIS ONE BEFORE
THE VIRUS MAN IS PLAYING TRICKS SOON WON'T BE ANY MORE
CALL THE DISC DOCTOR BACKAGAIN
HE'S BOUND TO KNOW THE ANSWER
WITH MR RAM THE MEMORY MAN THEY'LL FIX THIS
VIRUSDANCER.

SWARTHY BILL

A PIRATE BOLD WITH RINGS OF GOLD
HIS NAME WAS SWARTHY BILL
WITH SEVEN NOTCHES ON HIS BELT
AND SEVEN MORE MEN TO KILL.

HE'D SAILED THE SEA FROM MANY A SHORE
AND WAS FEARED BY OH SO MANY
HIS HEART WAS BLACK AS BLACK COULD BE
COMPASSION HE HAD NOT ANY.

I MET THIS PIRATE BOLD ONE DAY
WHILE SAILING ROUND THE OCEAN
HE CAME ABOARD MY SHIP AND SAID
HANDS UP YOUR GOLD AND THAT THERE POTION.

I GAVE THE POTION TO HIM
BUT LITTLE DID HE KNOW
THAT WHEN HE DRANK THE POTION
HIS MEMORY IT WOULD GO.

SO NOW HE SAILS THE OCEAN
BUT NO ONE FEARS HIS NAME
FOR SWARTHY BILLS A BROKEN MAN
SINCE HE LOST HIS CLAIM TO FAME.

TELL ME

LISTEN TO THE FALLING RAIN
TELL ME WHAT YOU HEAR
CAN YOU HEAR IT CRYING
CAN YOU SEE ATEAR.

SMELL THE FLOWERS GROWING
ROSES FILL THE AIR
CAN YOU SMELL THEIR PERFUME
DRIFTING EVERYWHERE.

FEEL THE THINGS THAT MATTER
FORGET THE THINGS THAT DON'T
THEN YOU WILL BE HAPPY
EVEN THOUGH YOU THINK YOU WON'T.

THE UNIVERSE

HAVE YOU EVER WATCHED A STAR AT NIGHT
SEEN HOW BEAUTIFUL IT GLEAMS
SO NEAR AND YET SO FAR AWAY
I SEE THEM IN MYDREAMS.

IN THE EVENING AIR WHEN ALL IS STILL
AND DAY HAS TURNED TO NIGHT
I'D LOVE TO CLIMB UP TO A STAR
AND LET MY WINGS TAKE FLIGHT.

THE MYSTERY OF THE UNIVERSE
IT BECKONS FROM AFAR
WITH ALL ITS HIDDEN SECRETS
SUCH BEAUTY IN THE SKY.

THE DOWN AND OUT

TIRED AND WEARY NO PLACE TO GO
GOT A SINKING FEELING WAY DOWN BELOW
THE BOTTLE IS EMPTY I'VE SUPPED THE LAST DROP
HAVE TO MOVE ON HEAR THE SOUND OF A COP

A SHED OR A BENCH WILL DO ME JUST FINE
BE ABLE TO SLEEP TILL AROUND ABOUT NINE
MY HANDS ARE SO COLD NOBODYS IN SIGHT
AND DREADING THE THOUGHT OF THIS LONELY NIGHT.

TOMORROW AGAIN I'LL BE OFF ON A SPREE
WHY DID I CHOOSE THIS LIFE FOR ME
NO ONE TO LOVE ME NO ONE TO CARE
NOBODY WAITING AT HOME IN A CHAIR.

I'M TOO OLD NOW TO MEND MY WAYS
I'LL BE WALKING THE STREETS FOR THE REST OF MY DAYS
SOMEONE WILL FIND ME SPRAWLED OUT ON A SEAT
WITH A BOTTLE OF WHISKY CLOSE BY AT MY FEET.

THE GREATEST TREASURE

MY WORLD IS FILLED WITH SUNSHINE
WHEN YOU ARE CLOSE TO ME
I SEE THE STARS UP IN THE SKY
THE LEAVES UPON A TREE.

WHY CAN'T WE STAY FOREVER
IN THIS HEAVEN WE HAVE FOUND
LET THE WORLD GO PASSING BY
LISTEN, NOT ASOUND.

FOR YOU ARE ALL I LONG FOR
YOU ARE ALL I NEED
LOOK THE FLOWERS IN AGREEMENT
NOD THEIR HEADS TO ME.

LOVES THE GREATEST TREASURE
THAT ANYONE CAN HOLD
WITHOUT IT YOU ARE NOTHING
YOU WITHER AND GROWOLD.

THE LONG ROAD

THERE'S A LIGHT SHINING BRIGHT UP ABOVE ME
THERE'S A VOICE EVER CALLING MY NAME
ON THAT LONG ROAD THAT STRETCHES BEFORE US
IN MEMORY IT'S ALWAYS THE SAME.

THE FLOWERS GROW TALL ALL AROUND ME
AS I WALK NEATH THE SUNSHINE ABOVE
AND A LITTLE BIRD SINGING SO SWEETLY
ITS MELODIC SONG OFLOVE.

I THRILL TO THE BEAUTY AROUND ME
IN AWE FOR THIS HAVEN I'VE FOUND
THE TREES STANDING TALL SEEM TO WHISPER
AS THE LEAVES FLOAT SOFT TO THE GROUND.

I MUST FOLLOW THE LIGHT THAT IS SHINING
IT WILL LEAD ME STRAIGHT TO YOU
DOWN THAT ROAD THAT STRETCHES BEFORE ME
PARADISE HEAVEN AND YOU.

THE ROSE

I PLANTED A ROSE IN MY GARDEN
A RED RED ROSE OF LOVE
I WATCHED IT SLOWLY GROWING
AS THE SUN SHONE HIGH ABOVE.

THE ROSE I PLANTED JUST FOR YOU
TO TELL YOU HOW I CARE
AND WHEN YOU SEE IT BLOSSOMING
YOU WILL KNOW THAT I AM THERE .

THE SMILE

BEHIND THE SMILE LIES SADNESS
WITHIN THE EYES A TEAR
BEYOND THE LAUGHTER, HEARTACHE
WITHIN THE SOULDEFEAT.

ABOVE THE RAIN THERE'S SUNSHINE
WITHIN THE HEART THERE'S LOVE
ABOVE THE EARTH THERE'S HEAVEN
AND SUNSHINE UPABOVE.

THE STRANGER

A STRANGER SPOKE TO ME TODAY
AND YET I KNEW HIM WELL
SOMETHING IN HIS EYES I SAW
THOUGH WHAT I COULD NOT TELL.

HE SMILED AND SAID GOOD MORNING
IT TOOK ME BY SURPRISE
HE SMILED A SMILE SO KNOWING
SO FRIENDLY AND SO WISE.

A FEELING OF WARMTH SWEPT OVER ME
I WATCHED HIM WALK ONBY
I KNEW THAT HE WAS WATCHING ME
AND YET I DID NOT KNOW WHY.

I WANTED TO TURN AND FOLLOW HIM
MY HEART WAS BEATING FAST
I TURNED AROUND BUT HE WAS GONE
AND I KNEW THAT JESUS HAD PASSED.

THE WORLD IS NOT AS IT SHOULD BE

INTO THIS WORLD CAME A MAN
FOLLOWING CAME A WOMAN
ALL AROUND WAS BEAUTY
ALL AROUND WAS CALM
THEN THERE CAMECALAMITY
AS THE SERPENT WEAVED ITS CHARM.

THE WORLD WAS NOT AS IT SHOULD BE
AND MAN BEGAN TO SIN
WITH TURMOIL AND DISOBEDIENCE
EVERYONE FIGHTING TO WIN.

SO GOD DECIDED TO CHANGE THINGS
TEACH THE WORLD HOW TO LIVE
HE PREACHED ABOUT THE GOSPELS
HE TAUGHT MAN HOW TO GIVE.

AND SO AS LIFE IS TURNING
WE THINK ON WHAT HE SAID
IF ONLY WE WOULD FOLLOW
THE TEACHINGS THAT WERE READ.

WHAT WHERE WHO

WHERE ARE YOU GOING TO
WITH YOUR STEP SO GAY
I'M GOING TO MEET THE FISHING BOATS
ARRIVING IN THE BAY.

WHO DO YOU HOPE TO SEE
WHEN THE MEN COME IN
I HOPE TO SEE MY LOVER BOY
AND HIS HEART TO WIN.

WHAT WILL YOU SAY TO HIM
AS HE STEPS ASHORE
I'LL SAY TO HIM I LOVE YOU
HE'LL SAY I'LL LEAVE NO MORE.

WILL YOU BUY

THERE CAME A YOUNG GIRL CALLING
KNOCK KNOCKING AT MY DOOR
HER EYES WERE DARK AND SMOULDERING
BUY SOME SHELLS, FROM OFF THE SHORE.

I LOOKED INSIDE HER BASKET
AND THERE TO MY SURPRISE
WERE COLOURED SHELLS AND ORNAMENTS
OF EVERY SHAPE AND SIZE.

HER CLOTHES WERE TORN AND RAGGED
HER CHEEKS WERE WHITE AS SNOW
AND PEEPING THROUGH HERSANDALS
I COULD SEE HER LITTLE TOE.

WILL YOU BUY FROM ME PLEASE LADY
SHE SOFTLY SAID TO ME
I ANSWERED VERY QUICKLY
COME IN AND HAVE SOME TEA.

SHE SAT DOWN BESIDE THE FIRE
AND A TEAR BEGAN TOFALL
I LOOKED AT HER, AND ASKED HER
WHY DID YOU REALLYCALL.

WELL I'M THE CHILD YOU LEFT BEHIND
THE ONE YOU DID NOTKEEP
I'VE COME TO FIND YOU MOTHER
AND THEY BOTH BEGAN TO WEEP.

YOU CAN'T COME IN HERE

YOU CAN'T COME IN HERE, SAID THE DOORMAN
DRESSED IN HIS TOP TAILS AND HAT
WHY NOT, I ANSWERED POLITELY
BECAUSE YOU CAN'T AND THAT'S THAT.

I LOOKED DOWN AT MY CREASED BAGGY TROUSERS
MY SHIRT HAD SEEN BETTER DAYS
I STUBBORNLY STOOD IN THE DOORWAY
WHILE THE DOORMAN SAID SCAT, GO AWAY.

NOW I'M USUALLY A QUITE GENTLE FELLA
AND DON'T LIKE A FUSS OR A SCENE
BUT HE REALLY GOT UNDER MY COLLAR
WITH HIS TOFFY NOSED MANNER SO MEAN.

SO I TRIED ONCE MORE TO GAIN ENTRANCE
BUT HE WAS HAVING NONE OF THAT
SO I WALKED RIGHT UP TO HIM DEFTLY
WITH ONE BLOW KNOCKED HIM FLAT ON HIS BACK.

A NEWWORLD

I WROTE OF LOVE AND TRAGEDY
I WROTE OF WAR ANDHATE
I LISTENED TO THE MELODIES
I LISTENED TO THE RAIDS.

THE WORLD HAS COME FULL CIRCLE
THE WINDS OF LIFE DON'T CHANGE
AND ALL THE TIME ITS RAINING
I'M STANDING IN THE RAIN.

I THOUGHT ABOUT A NEW WORLD
A WORLD WHERE NONE WOULD CRY
BRIGHT COLOURS OF THE RAINBOW
GO DANCING IN THE SKY.

SOMEWHERE IN ALL THIS DARKNESS
A STAR SHINES HIGH ABOVE
THE NEW WORLD THAT I THOUGHT ABOUT
IS HEAVEN UP ABOVE.

ACROSS THAT BRIDGE

ACROSS THAT BRIDGE OF NO RETURN
WHERE ANGELS FEAR TO TREAD
WHERE CLOUDS ROLL BY IN CLUSTERS
AND CHILDREN SLEEP IN BED.

ACROSS THAT BRIDGE IS WAITING
A WORLD UNKNOWN TO MAN
FOR WE ARE BUT MERE MORTALS
IN THIS MASTERPLAN.

ACROSS THAT BRIDGE LIES THE ANSWER
TO HOW, WHERE ANDWHY
THE REASON FOR OUR LIVING
THE REASON WHY WEDIE.

ANSWERS LEFT UNSPOKEN

TEARS UPON MY PILLOW
SMILES UPON MY FACE
HIDDEN DREAMS,AND HEARTACHES
PROMISES MADE OF LACE.

PICTURES IN MY MEMORY
TREACHERY AND LIES
ANSWERS LEFT UNSPOKEN
LOVE THAT NEVER DIES.

PATHS THAT WE HAVE TAKEN
THOUGHTS THAT WE HAVE HAD
WILL REMAINFOREVER
TO MAKE US FEELSAD.

BUT LIFE IS TO BE LIVED
AND LESSONS TO BE LEARNED
SO TEARS AND SMILES AND DREAMS
ARE BRIDGES TO BE BURNED.

BIG SHIPS SMALL SHIPS

UPON THE CLIFF TOP HIGH
I LOOK DOWN AT THESEA
THE BOATS ARE IN THE HARBOUR
THEY WAIT FOR YOU AND ME.

BIG SHIPS AND SMALL SHIPS
THEY ALL GO SAILING BY
OUT INTO THE OCEAN
WHERE THE SEABIRDS CRY.

FAR AWAY OUT THEY SAIL
TO FAR OFF DISTANT SHORES
OUT INTO THE DARK NIGHT
HEAR THE SEA THAT ROARS.

FAIRIES

AT NIGHT WHEN WE ARE SLEEPING
AND EVERYTHING IS STILL
ALL THE LITTLE FAIRIES
COME FLYING DOWN THEHILL.

THEY GATHER IN THE GARDENS
AND UNDERNEATH THETREES
THEY DANCE AND SING TILL MORNING
AND FLUTTER IN THE BREEZE.

LITTLERABBITS

THREE LITTLE RABBITS SITTING ALL ALONE
THEY WERE VERYHUNGRY
AND HAD LOST THEIR WAY HOME
SO I SAID COME ON FOLLOW ME
I WILL GET YOUTHERE.

BUT FIRST I'LL FIND A CARROT
ONE THAT YOU CAN SHARE
THEY HOPPED AND THEY JUMPED
AND SEEMED HAPPY AS COULD BE
AND I SAID GOODBYE AND HURRIED HOME FOR TEA.

FOLLOW THAT STAR

FOLLOW THAT STAR
THE ONE HIGH ABOVE
ITS SHINING FOR YOU
FROM HEAVEN WITH LOVE.

CAPTURE THAT MOONBEAM
SEE HOW IT GLOWS
TREAD VERY CAREFULLY
SO NOBODY KNOWS.

DANCE WITH THE SUNSHINE
HAPPY AND GAY
DON'T LET THE RAINDROPS
WASH YOU AWAY.

PLAY WITH THE FAIRIES
OUT IN THE DEW
THEY ARE JUST WAITING
WAITING FOR YOU.

LOOK UP TO HEAVEN
WHAT DO YOU SEE
RUBIES AND EMERALDS
FOR YOU AND FOR ME.

I WILL ALWAYS LOVE YOU

I KNOW YOU'LL FORGET ME WHEN I'VE GONE
OH YOU LOVE ME NOW THAT'S TRUE
BUT DAY BY DAY AS LOVE GROWS COLD
AND I REMEMBER YOU
I'LL BE JUST A MEMORY SOMEBODY YOU ONCE KNEW.

MY PHOTOGRAPH WILL STILL BE THERE
BUT I WILL BE FAR AWAY
AND YOU WILL FIND SOMEBODY ELSE
TO GET YOU THROUGH YOUR DAY.

BUT I WILL ALWAYS LOVE YOU
TILL THE STARS NO LONGER SHINE
AND IN ANOTHER TIME AND PLACE
YOU WILL STILL BE MINE.

LET ME DREAM

LET ME WALK UPON YOUR SANDY SHORE
LET ME BREATHE YOUR SALTY AIR
WHERE THE SEAGULLSCRY
AS A BOAT SAILS BY
SOMEWHERE OVER THERE.

LET ME SIT UNDERNEATH A STARLIT SKY
LET ME DREAM OF A NEW TOMORROW
WHERE THE WORLD WILL BE
FOR YOU AND FOR ME
A WORLD WITH NO MORE SORROW.

LET ME HOLD YOU CLOSE EVER TIGHTLY
LET ME TELL YOU HOW I LOVE YOU
WHERE THE FLOWERSGROW
BY THE SWEET HEDGEROWS
AND THE SKY ABOVE ISBLUE.

LISTEN

LISTEN TO THE VOICE INSIDE
IT'S TELLING YOU HAVEPITY
SPARE A THOUGHT FOR THOSE IN NEED
LIVING IN CARDBOARDCITY.

LISTEN TO THE BEGGAR
WHO WANDERS AROUND THE STREET
PUT YOUR HAND IN YOUR PURSE
AND HELP HIM TO HIS FEET.

LISTEN TO THE CRYING
OF THOSE WHO HAVE LOST THEIR WAY
MAYBE YOU CAN GIVE THEM HOPE
TO FACE ANOTHER DAY.

LISTEN TO THE UNIVERSE
BEFORE IT IS TO LATE
DO WHATEVER YOU CAN DO
DO IT NOW DON'T WAIT.

MAKE BELIEVE

THERE IS A LAND OF MAKE BELIEVE
WHERE ALL YOUR DREAMS COME TRUE
IT'S ONLY OVER THE RAINBOW
AND WAITING THERE FOR YOU.

IF YOU CLOSE YOUR EYES AND LISTEN
SWEET MUSIC FILLS THE AIR
ALL AROUND A GOLDEN GLOW
IS SHININGEVERYWHERE.

JUST CLOSE THE DOOR BEHIND YOU
MOVE FORWARD TO THE LIGHT
FEEL THE WARMTH AROUND YOU
GO GENTLY TO THENIGHT.

THERE IS A LAND OF MAKE BELIEVE
I KNOW CAUSE I'VE BEEN THERE
AND SOMEDAY YOU WILL FIND IT
WHEN YOUR HEART IS FREE OF CARE.

TEARS UPON MY PILLOW

FLOWERS BY THE HEDGEROW
BIRDS UP IN THESKY
RIPPLES BY A WATERFALL
PEOPLE PASSINGBY.

SHIPS UPON THE OCEAN
MEN WHO GO TO WAR
POEMS LONG FORGOTTEN
DON'T HEAR THEM ANYMORE.

STARS THAT SHINE SO BRIGHTLY
LEAVES THAT SOFTLY FALL
SHADOWS ON THE CEILING
PICTURES ON A WALL.

TEARS UPON MY PILLOW
WORDS THAT WERE UNTRUE
HEARTS THAT LOVE FOREVER
LOVING ONLY YOU.

THANKYOU

WHILE STARS ARE IN THE SKY AT NIGHT
AND THE SUN SHINES IN THE DAY
WHEN ALL THE WORLDS FORGOTTEN
I'LL LOOK UP TO GOD ANDPRAY.

THANK YOU FOR MY BEGINNING
THANK YOU FOR BEING A FRIEND
THANK YOU FOR ALWAYS BEING THERE
MY THANK YOU'S HAVE NO END.

IF I SHOULD DIE TOMORROW
THE WORLD WOULD CARE NOT FOR ME
BUT AS LONG AS YOU ARE BESIDE ME
I'LL SAY THANK YOU ETERNALLY.

THE JOKER

A GREAT BIG SMILE UPON HIS FACE
BUT IN HIS EYES THERE'S PAIN
HE LAUGHS AND JOKES WITH EVERYONE
AS HE PLAYS HIS PART AGAIN.

FOR NO ONE KNOWS HIS MISERY
THE HEART THAT LOVED IN VAIN
HIS LONELY NIGHTS AND EMPTY DAYS
BRING NOTHING MORE THAN RAIN.

HOW LONG CAN HE ENDURE THIS LIFE
WITH NO ONE BY HIS SIDE
FOR SHE TOOK EVERYTHING HE HAD
SHE TOOK AWAY HIS PRIDE.

AND SO HE SMILES AND CARRIES ON
HIS LIFE AS JUSTBEFORE
THOUGH EVERYTHING IN LIFE HAS GONE
LONELINESS EVERMORE.

THE BAND STARTS UP THE LIGHTS GO DOWN
THE AUDIENCE WAITING THERE
WITHOUT A SOUND HE WANDERS ON
DOES NOT ANYBODY CARE.

THE DAY GOD CAME TO CALL

NO ONE KNEW OR UNDERSTOOD.
OR EVER EVEN CARED
ABOUT A HEART SO BROKEN
THAT COULD NOT BE REPAIRED.

LOVE WAS ALL IT HAD TO GIVE
LOVE FOR ALL TO SHARE
NO ONE SAW THE LONELINESS
THE SADNESS LIVING THERE.

FAINTER AS THE YEARS WENT BY
DISHEARTENED BY IT ALL
IT SUDDENLY STOPPED BEATING
THE DAY GOD CAME TO CALL.

THE MAN WITH THE GOLDEN HEART

SO QUIETLY HE LIVED HIS LIFE
IN THE BACKGROUND ALWAYS THERE
NO FUSS OR FAVOURS HE DID ASK
YET SHOWED THAT HE DID CARE.

HIS LOVE WAS GIVEN FREELY
THOUGH NONE EVER SAID IT SO
THROUGH ALL HIS TRIBULATIONS
HE HAD TO STAND ALONE.

HE HAD NO FRIEND TO HELP HIM
NO PARTNER BY HIS SIDE
HIS DAYS WERE LONG AND LONELY
BUT YET HE STRUGGLEDBY.

BETRAYAL ALL AROUND HIM
NO ONE EVER UNDERSTOOD
OR EVER EVEN CARED
ABOUT A HEART SO BROKEN
IT COULD NOT BEREPAIRED.

THE ROSY RED APPLE

THE APPLE TREE SO TEMPTING
WITH ITS JUICY APPLES RED
NO ONE CAN RESISTTHEM
SO IT HAS BEEN SAID.

BUT I KNOW A SECRET
THE WAY TO SAY NO
DON'T TRY TO BITE IT
TURN AROUND AND GO.

FOR THE ROSY RED APPLE
WILL ONLY BRING YOU PAIN
IF YOU CAN RESIST IT
IT WILL NOT BE IN VAIN.

THE EMPTY ROOM

HE LOOKED AROUND THE EMPTY ROOM
SO MANY MEMORIES THERE
AS HE REMEMBERED ALL THOSE YEARS
NOW IT LOOKED SO BARE.

THE CREAKING OF A FLOORBOARD
THE ONE HE MEANT TO MEND
SOMEHOW HE NEVER GOT ROUND TO IT
HE LENT HIS TOOLS TO HIS FRIEND.

A LIKELY TALE HE TOLD HIMSELF
JUST ANOTHER EXCUSE
LIKE THE TIME HE MEANT TO PAINT THE DOOR
THE LAZINESS PROFUSE.

NOW ALL HE HAD WERE MEMORIES
FOR HE WAS GROWING OLD
HE LOOKED ONCE MORE AROUND THE EMPTY ROOM
IT LOOKED SO BARE AND COLD.

THE STRANGE MAN

A STRANGE MAN CAME A KNOCKING
A KNOCKING AT MY DOOR
HE ASKED ME COULD I TELL HIM
THE WAY TO DONEGAL.

HIS EYES WERE BRIGHT AND MERRY
HIS VOICE WAS DEEP AND STRONG
HE ASKED ME IF I'D LISTEN
TO HIS LILTING IRISHSONG.

AND AS HE SANG I LISTENED
I THOUGHT I SAW HIMSMILE
HE TIPPED HIS HAT AND VANISHED
AND I WAS LEFTBEGUILED.

THE TEARDROP

IT FELL UPON A PETAL
THEN FELL UPON THE GROUND
AND AS IT SLOWLYLANDED
IT DID NOT MAKE ASOUND.

IT CAME FROM OUT OF NOWHERE
OR FROM THE SKY ABOVE
I ONLY KNOW THAT SOMEWHERE
THE AIR WAS FILLED WITH LOVE.

I LOOKED AROUND AND LISTENED
SAW A GIRL GO WALKING BY
AND AS SHE TURNED A TEARDROP
WAS GLISTENING IN HER EYE.

TRAVELLING

I SAW A STAR ABOVE ME
IT SPARKLED AND IT SHONE
IT TOOK ME ON A JOURNEY
TO WHERE NO MORTALS GONE.

IT SHOWED TO ME A PATHWAY
SO FAR UP IN THE SKY
AND I WAS CLOSE BEHIND IT
I WAS TRAVELLING SOHIGH.

THE FEELING WAS ENTRANCING
AS I WENT FLOATING BY
LOOKING DOWN BELOWME
AT PEOPLE PASSING BY.

IT SEEMED TOLASTFOREVER.
SOMEWHERE OUT THERE IN SPACE
AND I WAS PART OF THE UNIVERSE
IN ANOTHER TIME ANDPLACE.

WHEN YOU ARE FAR AWAY

WHEN ALL THE WORLD HAS GONE TO SLEEP
AND YOU ARE FAR AWAY
I THINK OF YOU MY DARLING
EACH AND EVERY DAY.

I SEE YOU NEATH THE MOONLIGHT
I HEAR YOU WHISPER LOW
AND WHEN THE NIGHT IS OVER
YOUR MEMORY STILL WONT GO.

YOUR CLOSE BESIDE ME ALWAYS
NO MATTER WHAT I DO
AND TILL THE DAY YOUR HOME AGAIN
I'LL ALWAYS BE LOVING YOU.

WHY

WHY DO WE LOSE ALL THAT WE LOVE
WHY ARE THERE CLOUDS IN THE SKY
SURELY THE WORLD WAS NOT MEANT TO BE SO
WHY DO WE LIVE AND THEN DIE.

THERE'S GOT TO BE A REASON FOR THIS
ONLY GOD IN HIS HEAVEN KNOWS WHY
THE WORLD WAS MEANT TO BE BEAUTIFUL
AND WE WEREN'T BORN TOCRY.

IT MUST BE MAN WHO SPOILT IT
TURNED LOVING INTO HATE
FOR ALL OF US ARESINNERS
AS WE SERVE OUR TIME THEN WAIT.

BUT IN THE SWEET HEREAFTER
GOD HAS WELCOME ARMS
AND THOSE WHO TRULY LOVE HIM
WILL HAVE THE PEACE THAT CALMS.

YESTERDAYS GONE FOREVER

IT'S A LONG AND LONELY JOURNEY
THROUGH THIS MAZE WERE LIVING IN
THE DARKNESS HANGS AROUND US
THE WORLD IS FULL OF SIN.

YESTERDAYS GONE FOREVER
TOMORROW MAY NEVER BE
I HEAR THE CALL OF THE SEABIRD
DOES HE SING HIS SONG TO ME.

IT'S A LONG AND LONELY JOURNEY
TILL THIS LIFE ON EARTH IS THROUGH
BUT SOMEWHERE IN THE DARKNESS
I WILL COME TO YOU.

YOU SO BRAVE

YOU STAND SO BRAVE
YOUR HEAD HELD HIGH
I'LL TREATED YOU HAVE BEEN
THE WHITE MAN CAME TO CONQUER
THE WHITE MAN CAME TOSTEAL.

HE TOOK AWAY YOUR LAND FROM YOU
AND TRIED TO TAKE YOURPRIDE
BUT YOU STOOD TALL THROUGHOUT IT ALL
WITH YOUNG BRAVES SIDE BY SIDE.

SO NOW YOU FIERCELY DEFEND
WHAT LAND YOU HAVE GOT LEFT
AND I FOR ONE UNDERSTAND
HOW YOU SHOULD FEEL BEREFT.

POVERTY

LIVING IN A THREE ROOMED SHACK
NO FOOD UPON THE TABLE
SLEEPING ON A DIRTY SACK
WITH JIMMY, AND OUR MABEL.

LIFE WAS TOUGH, WHEN WE WERE YOUNG
ME DAD DRUNK ALL THE MONEY
ME MOTHER ONLY HAD ONE LUNG
AND LIFE WEREN'T VERYFUNNY.

THE WATER LEAKED IN EVERY WHERE
AND IT SMELT DANK ANDMUSTY
A CRUST OF BREAD, WEDE HAVE TO SHARE
AND SOMETIMES IT WASFUSTY.

OFT WE HAD NO SHOES TO WEAR
AND NOTHING IN OUR BELLIES
BUT WE WERE YOUNG AND DID NOT CARE
WE ALWAYS HAD OUR WELLIES.

MOTHER DIED OF A BROKEN HEART
WITH NOTHING TO HER NAME
ME DAD WAS CARRIED OFF IN A CART
TO EVERYBODY'S SHAME.

NOW JIMMY AND OURMABLE
HAVE GONE THERE SEPARATE WAYS
SO LET'S OPEN UP ABOTTLE
AND REMEMBER THE GOOD OLD DAYS.

IN BLUEBELL WOOD

IN BLUEBELL WOOD SHE FELL IN LOVE
HER HEART WAS YOUNG AND GAY
SHE SAW THOSE EYES, WAS MESMERIZED
BUT THEN HE WENT AWAY.

WITH WORDS OF LOVE, HE TOOK HER HAND
AND WHISPERED, PLEASE BE MINE
AND ALL THE STARS IN HEAVEN
WILL LOOK DOWN ON US ANDSHINE.

OH, YES SHE ANSWERED SWEETLY
I'D GIVE MY LIFE FOR YOU
THERE'S NOTHING IN THIS WORLD
I WOULD NOT DO FORYOU.

SURROUNDED BY THE BLUEBELLS
AND A STREAM THAT TRICKLED BY
LET'S STAY HERE FOREVER
THIS WAS MEANT FOR YOU AND I.

BUT NOW SHE WALKS ALONE
THROUGH THE BLUEBELLS AND HEATHER
FOR HER LOVE, HE FOUND ANOTHER
NOW THEY WILL NEVER BETOGETHER.

ROSEMARY BLACK

AT THE END OF THE ROAD, IN A LONELY OLD SHACK
THERE ONCE LIVED A WOMAN CALLED ROSEMARY BLACK
SHE LIVED ALL ALONE, WITH HER OLD BLACK CAT
HER ONLY VISITOR AN ODD STRAY RAT.

SHE WAS NEVER SEEN WHEN IT WAS LIGHT
BUT SHE WOULD COME OUT IN THE DEAD OF NIGHT
SOME PEOPLE OFTEN WONDERED WHY
THEY EVEN SAID THEY HAD SEEN HER FLY.

THE RUMOURS CAME AS RUMOURS DO
AND NO ONE KNEW IF THEY WERE TRUE
THEY BLAMED HER FOR THIS,AND BLAMED HER FOR THAT
THEY EVEN BLAMED HER OLD BLACK CAT.

ONE NIGHT THEY DECIDED TO SEE WHERE SHE WENT
SO THEY FOLLOWED THE OLD WOMAN CROOKED AND BENT
WITH HER OLD BLACK CAT FOLLOWING BEHIND
EVERY ONE WONDERED WHAT THEY WOULD FIND.

THEN UNDER A TREE NOT FAR AWAY
THE OLD WOMAN KNELT DOWN AND BEGAN TO PRAY
AND THERE IN THE MOONLIGHT FOR ALL TO SEE
WAS A BIG WOODEN CROSS FROM AN OLD OAK TREE.

FLOWERS OF EVERY SHAPE AND SIZE
THEY COULD HARDLY BELIEVE THEIR OWN TWO EYES
THEY LOOKED AT EACH OTHER WITH SHAME AND DISGUST
FOR BEING TO THE OLD WOMAN SOUNJUST.

NOT LONG AFTER THAT THE OLD WOMAN DIED
AND ONE OR TWO IN THE VILLAGE CRIED
THEN IN HER MEMORY THEY PUT UP A PLAQUE
HERE LIES THE BODY, OF SWEET ROSEMARYBLACK.

CHILD OF THE SUN

A CHILD OF THE SUN SO BEAUTIFUL
WITH HAIR OF GOLDEN HUE
SHE WALKS WITH RAYS OF SUNSHINE
NEATH SUMMER SKIES OF BLUE.

THE BIRDS ALL STOP THEIR SINGING
WHEN SHE GOES WALKING BY
SHE SINGS A GENTLE LILTING SONG
THE NOTES GO SOARING HIGH.

CHILD OF THE SUN SO BEAUTIFUL
YOU LEAVE A SPECIAL GLOW
YELLOW RAYS OF HAPPINESS
GENTLE BREEZES BLOW.

A NEW WORLD

I WROTE OF LOVE AND TRAGEDY
I WROTE OF WAR AND HATE
I LISTENED TO THE MELODIES
I LISTENED TO THE RAIDS.

THE WORLD HAS COME FULL CIRCLE
THE WINDS OF LIFE DON'T CHANGE
AND ALL THE TIME IT'S RAINING
I'M STANDING IN THE RAIN.

I THOUGHT ABOUT A NEW WORLD
A WORLD WHERE NONE WOULD CRY
BRIGHT COLOURS OF THE RAINBOW
GO DANCING IN THE SKY.

SOMEWHERE IN ALL THIS DARKNESS
A STAR SHINES HIGH ABOVE
THE NEW WORLD THAT I THOUGHT ABOUT
IS HEAVEN UP ABOVE.

MY SECRET GARDEN

I KNOW A LITTLE GARDEN
HIDDEN OUT OF SIGHT
WITH LITTLE PATHS AND ROCKERY
AND WATER TRICKLING BRIGHT.

IT HAS AN OLD STONE DOOR
WHO MADE IT, I DON'T KNOW
I USED TO TAKE MY DOLLS THERE
MANY YEARS AGO.

IT WAS MY SECRET GARDEN
I FOUND IT WHILE PLAYING AROUND
I USED TO THINK NOBODY ELSE KNEW
THIS GARDEN I HAD FOUND.

AND WHEN THE SCHOOL WAS OVER
I'D HURRY HOME FOR TEA
CALLING FOR MY BEST FRIEND
SAYING, DO YOU WANT TO COME WITH ME!.

WE'D COLLECT OUR DOLLS AND HURRY
TO OUR VERY SECRET PLACE
THEN SIT ON A LITTLE WOODEN SEAT
SEE THE REFLECTION OF A FACE.

ITS MANY YEARS AGO NOW
AND I SELDOM GO THAT WAY
BUT I'M SURE MY SECRET GARDEN
IS STILL STANDING THERE TODAY.

VISIONS

IN THE DARKENED SKY I SEE
VISIONS OF ETERNITY
HOPE AND DREAMS OF LIFE TO COME
LIVING IN ETERNAL SUN.

I STAND TRANSFIXED AT THE WONDER
THE STARS THAT SHINE SO BRIGHT
THE HEAVENLY BREEZE THAT'S BLOWING
SOMEWHERE IN THE NIGHT.

ONE STEP BEYOND THE CLOUDS ABOVE
AWAITS A SCEPTERED ISLE OF LOVE
THE RUSTLE OF AN ANGEL'S WINGS
HUSH, I HEAR A BIRD THATSINGS!

FLOATING GENTLY TO THAT LIGHT
MY SOUL HAS TAKEN FLIGHT
I KNOW AT LAST, I'VE REACHED MY GOAL
FOR I'M IN PARADISE.

RARE BIRD

LITTLE BIRD SO SWEET AND RARE.
WOULD BUT I SET YOU FREE.
YOU WOULD FLY SO HIGH,
IN THE SKY. IF IT WERE UP TO ME.

BUT YOU MUST STAY WITHIN YOUR PRISON.
AND I MUST KEEP THE KEY.
I WONDER WOULD YOU THINK OF ME.
WERE I TO SET YOUFREE.

LITTLE BIRD YOU SING SO SWEETLY.
MANY ARE YOURCHARMS.
I'D LIKE TO OPEN UP YOUR DOOR,
AND FREE YOU FROM ALL HARM.

LITTLE BIRD YOU COULD NOT BE SAFE,
IN THE CRUEL WORLD OUTSIDE.
THAT'S WHY I KEEP YOU IN YOUR CAGE.
IT'S A PLACE FOR YOU TO HIDE.

LOOKING BACK

LOOKING BACK UPON MY LIFE
SO STRANGE NOW TO RECALL
FULL OF HAPPY MEMORIES
BESIDE THE GARDEN WALL.

WALLFLOWERS GROWING GAILY
LILAC TREES HANGING DOWN
GINGHAM AND CALICO LACES
NOT FORGETTING A RED VELVET GOWN.

OH! MANY'S THE TIME I GO WANDERING
DOWN THE LANES THAT ONCE I KNEW
WHERE PROFUSIONS OF DAISIES AND BLUEBELLS
I WOULD PICK, AND TAKE HOME AFEW.

THOSE DAYS WERE MY HAPPIEST MOMENTS
SPENT IN CHILDHOOD WAYS
SOMETHING I'LL ALWAYS REMEMBER
HOWEVER I SPEND MY DAYS.

WHO KNOWS

THE RAIN IS FALLING EVERYONE'S WET
HE JUST SITS THERE HAS NOT NOTICED IT YET
HIS HAIR IN STRAGGLES HANGING DOWN
AS HE SITS ON THE PAVEMENT IN THE CENTER OF TOWN.

AN OLD TATTERED COAT COVERS HIMUP
THEN HE TAKES A DRINK FROM A DIRTY OLD CUP
THE RAIN IS STILL FALLING SPLASHING AROUND
STILL HE SITS THERE MAKING NOSOUND!.

PEOPLE AROUND HIM ALL BUSTLING BY
CHILDREN POINTING AND QUESTIONING WHY
NO ONE CAN ANSWER THE REASON HE'STHERE
KNOW ONE WOULD ASK HIM THEY WOULD NOT DARE.

THE ONLY ANSWER THEY CAN EVER FIND
IS PUTTING HANDS IN THERE POCKETS AND BEING KIND
FOR WHO KNOWS ONE DAY IT COULD BE
SOMEBODY JUST LIKE YOU OR ME.

SOMEDAY

HOW COULD I EVER FORGET
THE ONE I LOVED SO MUCH
MY WORLD WAS FILLED WITH SUNSHINE
MY HEART WAS FILLED WITH LOVE.

NOW MY HEART IS LONELY
SINCE YOU WENT AWAY
THERE IS NO SUN TO SHINE ON ME
NO LAUGHTER IN MY DAY.

MAYBE SOMEDAY I'LL FIND YOU
TOGETHER WE WILL BE
LOST IN OUR LOVE FOREVER
WHERE THE HEAVENS MEET THE SEA.

LAND OF MAKE BELIEVE

LISTEN WHILE I TELL YOU
A STORY THAT IS TRUE
ABOUT THE LAND OF MAKE BELIEVE
AND A FAIRY DRESSED IN BLUE.

SHE CAME UPON MY WINDOW SILL
ONE BRIGHT AND STARRY NIGHT
SHE TWINKLED AND SHE SPARKLED
WITH A BLUE AND SILVERY LIGHT.

I WATCHED HER VERY CAREFULLY
THE AIR AROUND WAS STILL
AND THEN SHE BECKONED TO ME
I CAN NEVER FORGET THAT THRILL.

DON'T BE AFRAID MY LITTLE ONE
I AM YOUR FAIRYFRIEND
THEN IN A TWINKLE SHE WAS GONE
NOW MY STORY'S AT AN END.

SHE LOOKED THE OTHER WAY

WITH WILD ABANDON HE KISSED HER
AS SHE TREMBLED IN THE RAIN
HE TOLD HER HOW HE LOVED HER
COULD NOT WAIT TO SEE HER AGAIN.

HE GENTLY LAID HER DOWN
NEATH THE SUMMER SKY THAT DAY
AND AS THEY LAY IN SWEET CONTENT
SHE LOOKED THE OTHER WAY.

FOR SHE BELONGED TO SOMEONE ELSE
TO HIM SHE'D BEEN UNTRUE
SHE THOUGHT ABOUT TOMORROW
WHAT WAS SHE GOING TO DO.

THE ONLY THING SHE COULD DO
SAY GOODBYE AND QUICKLY GO
AND HOPE WITH ALL HER HEART
THAT HER LOVE WOULD NEVER KNOW.

MEMORIES OF THE NIGHT

TEARS OF SLEEP UPON MY FACE
MEMORIES OF THE NIGHT
LOST IN TRANQUIL DREAMS OF YOU
BIRDS IN FEATHERED FLIGHT.

COLOURS OF THE RAINBOW
BECKON FROM AFAR
GOLD AND SILVER SPANGLES
SHINING LIKE A STAR.

MUSIC ALL AROUND ME
YOUR FACE LOOKS DOWN WITH LOVE
I WANT TO STAYFOREVER
WITH THE ANGELS UP ABOVE.

BUT I MUST LEAVE THIS BEAUTY
COME BACK TO EARTH ONCE MORE
UNTIL THE DAY YOU COME FOR ME
TO ENTER THROUGH THAT DOOR.

A WARRIOR BRAVE

A WARRIOR BRAVE CAME RIDING BY
ON HIS JET BLACK HORSE
BENEATH A BLUE BLUE SKY.

THE HORSES HOOFS WENT GALLOPING ON
IN A BLINDING FLASH
THEY SOON WERE GONE.

AROUND THE BEND AND UP THE CREEK
FEATHERS FLYING
UPON PAINTED CHEEKS.

HE NEITHER LOOKED TO LEFT OR RIGHT
HIS FACE INTENT
SILHOUETTED IN THE LIGHT.

SOMEONE HAD DONE THE WARRIOR WRONG
HE WOULD FIND THAT MAN
AND IT WOULDN'T TAKE LONG.

FOR INDIANS ARE BRAVE AND PROUD
ESPECIALLY THIS ONE
KNOWN AS YOUNG GREY CLOUD.

A SHOT RANG THROUGH THE MORNING AIR
AND GREY CLOUD FELL
SOMEWHERE OVER THERE.

HE GOT ON HIS HORSE HEAD HELD HIGH
AND OFF THEY RODE
NEATH THE BLUE BLUE SKY.

STARRY NIGHT

FLICKERING SHADOWS ROUND THE ROOM
DANCING ON THECEILING
THOUGHTS GOING ROLLING ROUND MY HEAD
SUCH A LOVELYFEELING.

PEOPLE PASSING BY MY WINDOW
LIGHTS ARE SHINING BRIGHT
THE FIRES BURNING IN THE HEARTH
IT'S SUCH A STARRY NIGHT.

NEVER HAVE I FELT SUCH BLISS
THE REASON I DON'T KNOW
I ONLY KNOW I DIDN'T WANT
THIS NIGHT TO EVER GO.

MAYBE I WAS ON A JOURNEY
TO WHERE I COULDN'T TELL
BUT IN THE DISTANCE I COULD HEAR
A SONG I KNEW SO WELL.

AND NOW AS I LOOK BACK
TO THAT NIGHT SO LONG AGO
MAYBE I WAS DREAMING
I REALLY JUST DON'T KNOW.

WORLD OF WONDER

I SAW A WORLD OF WONDER
THE SKY A BRILLIANT BLUE
THE AIR IT SMELT OF WILD SWEET FLOWERS
AND STANDING THERE WAS YOU.

A GENTLE BREEZE BLEW ROUND ME
I HEARD AN ANGELSING
MY HEART AND MIND WENT SOARING
WITH THE BIRDS UPON THE WING.

NO DARKNESS TO ENFOLD ME
NO FEAR OF NIGHT HAD I
FOR EVERYTHING WAS FULL OF LIGHT
NO FEAR FOR THAT I MIGHT DIE.

A STAR SO BRIGHT AND SHINING
SEEMED TO SAY WITH LOVE
COME ON COME HERE BESIDE ME
YOUR WORLD IS HEREABOVE.

I SAW THIS PLACE OF WONDER
IT REALLY DID EXIST
AND THE AIR IT SMELT OF WILD SWEET FLOWERS
BEHIND THAT GENTLE MIST.

WHAT WILL I DO

WHAT WILL I DO,WHEN YOUR GONE FROM ME
HOW WILL I BEAR THE PAIN
FOR YOU ARE MY REASON FOR LIVING
YOU GAVE ME LIFE AGAIN.

WHERE WILL I GO WITHOUT YOU
WALKING AT MY SIDE
FOR MY LIFE WILL BE OVER
WITH YOU I WILL HAVE DIED.

WHEN ALL THE CRYINGS FINISHED
LIFE WILL STILL GO ON
I'LL HAVE NO REASON FOR LIVING
FOR ALL I LOVE WILL BE GONE.

THE HOUSE OF EVIL

I TURN AROUND BUT NO ONE IS THERE
JUST THE EERIE ROCKING OF AN OLD ROCKING CHAIR
THEN SUDDENLY ON THE STAIRS I SEE
A FORM THAT'S CALLING, CALLING TO ME.

I HURRY TO SEE WHAT IT'S ALL ABOUT
WHEN A THUNDEROUS VOICE SHOUTS GET OUT GET OUT
I GO TO THE TOP OF THE STAIRS ANDFIND
THE FRONT DOOR SLAMS AS I LOOK BEHIND.

A MOUSE SCUTTLES BY ON THE OLD WOODEN FLOOR
MAKING ITS WAY TO THE CLOSED FRONT DOOR
THE GHOSTLY HAND I SAW BEFORE
IS SLOWLY BECKONING ME ONCE MORE.

NEVER BEFORE HAVE I SEEN SUCH A SIGHT
A GHASTLY FIGURE DRESSED IN WHITE
WITH TWO BIG EYES IN A SKELETON HEAD
IT FILLS MY HEART WITH FEAR ANDDREAD.

NOW YOU'VE COME YOUR GOING TO STAY
YOU WON'T GET OUT OF HERE TODAY
AN EVIL SMILE LIT UP HIS FACE
MY HEART AND THOUGHTS BEGAN TO RACE.

AND THEN BEFORE MY VERY EYES
A HIDEOUS HOWL RANG THROUGH THE SKIES
I HAD TO GET OUT OF HERE ANDFAST
AS I LOOKED AT THIS THING WITH EYES AGHAST.

THE DOOR WAS LOCKED AND I TURNED THE KEY
WITH THE GHOSTLY FIGURE FOLLOWING ME
BEGONE IT SAID OR COME BACK AT YOUR PERIL
THAT GRUESOME FORM WITH THE FACE OF THE DEVIL.

LOVE GONE

MY LOVE WHY DO YOU STARE AT ME
FOR I HAVE DONE NO WRONG TO THEE.

YOUR EYES ARE COLD AND GONE THE GLOW
MY HEART IS SAD AND FULL OF WOE
GIVE ME THE LOVE WE USED TO KNOW
AND SMILE FOR ME BEFORE I GO
FOR YOU I LOVE WITH ALL MY HEART
AND PRAY THAT WE WILL NEVERPART.

MY LOVE WHY DO YOU STARE AT ME
FOR I HAVE DONE NO WRONG TOTHEE.

THE ONE WHO SEEMS TO LOSE

AM I TO BE FOREVER
BETRAYED BY ALL I MEET
LIVING A LIFE OF TORMENT
DEVOID OF ALL THAT'S SWEET.

WHY MUST I BE FOREVER
THE ONE WHO SEEMS TO LOSE
LIVING MY LIFE FOR OTHERS
WHY AREN'T I ALLOWED TO CHOOSE.

WHY AM I ALWAYS THE LOVER
NEVER THE ONE THAT'S LOVED
GIVING MY ALL TO SOMEONE
WHILE I GET PUSHED ANDSHOVED.

SOMEDAY IT'S GOT TO HAPPEN
SOMEONE WILL LOVE ME FOR ME
THEN I WILL FIND TRUE HAPPINESS
THE WAY IT WAS MEANT TO BE.

WILLOW TREE

WILLOW TREE OH WILLOW TREE
SO SADLY DO YOU WEEP
STANDING BY THE RIVERS EDGE
WHAT SECRETS DO YOU KEEP.

YOUR HEAD IS BOWED SO SWEETLY
I CAN NOT SEE YOUR FACE
I'D LIKE TO TAKE A PICTURE OF YOU
DRESSED IN GOSSAMER LACE.

YOUR BEAUTY IS BEYOND COMPARE
A QUEEN OF TREES ARE YOU
AND YET YOU BOW YOUR HEAD IN SORROW
ARE YOU UNHAPPY TOO.

WILLOW TREE OH WILLOW TREE
LOOK UP TOWARDS THE SKY
SO EVERYONE SEES YOUR LOVELINESS
AS THEY GO PASSING BY.

LOOKING FOR THE ANSWERS

THE PATH OF LIFE'S NOT EASY
AS YOU WEND YOUR WEARY WAY
LOOKING FOR THE ANSWERS
EACH AND EVERYDAY.

SHALL I GO THIS WAY, SHALL I GO THAT
IT'S NEVER EASY TO CHOOSE
AND IF YOU GO THE WRONG WAY
YOUR THE ONE TO LOSE.

ONE PATH IS THE RIGHT PATH
THE OTHER FULL OF WOE
YOU WANT TO FIND THE RIGHT PATH
BUT HOW ARE YOU TO KNOW.

THE FINAL PATH WE WALK UPON
IS VERY PLAIN TO TELL
ONE PATH LEADS TO HEAVEN
AND THE OTHER LEADS TO HELL.

WINTER WINDS

BLOW OH BLOW YOU WINTER WINDS
SPREAD YOUR SEEDS AROUND
AND I WILL WATCH THE SPINNING LEAVES
FLOATING TO THE GROUND.

MOAN AND GROAN DO YOUR WORST
BUT I WILL TAKE NO HARM
FOR AS YOU HURTLE THROUGH THE TREES
MY HEART WILL STILL STAY CALM.

BLOWING DOWN THE CHIMNEYS
WHISTLING THROUGH THE DOOR
IT IS WAY PASSED MIDNIGHT
I CAN'T HEAR YOU ANYMORE.

BLOW OH BLOW YOU WINTER WINDS
FOR SOON THE SPRING WILL COME
AND YOU WILL BE FORGOTTEN
AND THE HUMMING BIRD WILL HUM.

SOMEBODY IS YOU

THE NIGHT AIR DRIFTS AROUND ME
THE LIGHTS HAVE ALL GONE OUT
AS I WANDER HOME AT MIDNIGHT
NOT A SOUL IS THERE ABOUT.

JUST A TRICKLE OF SOME WATER
AS IT RUNS IN TO A DRAIN
AND A GARDEN GATE IS BANGING
FURTHER DOWN THE LANE.

THE MOON IS PEEPING SHYLY
FROM BEHIND A CLOUD ABOVE
AND I REMEMBER LONG AGO
YOU AND ME AND LOVE.

SUDDENLY I AM WARMER
AND MY HOUSE COMES IN TO VIEW
SOMEONE'S STANDING AT THE DOOR
AND THAT SOMEBODY IS YOU.

SHE SAT AND GAZED INTO THE FIRE

SHE SAT AND GAZED INTO THE FIRE
HER THOUGHTS WERE ALL OF HIM
HER HANDS WERE COLD, BUT A HEART WAS WARM
AS THE COALS IN THE FIRE GREW DIM.

SHE HEARD THE SOUNDS OF THE WIND OUTSIDE
AND REMEMBERED THE DAY HER DARLING DIED
A TEAR BEGAN TO TRICKLE DOWN HER FACE
AND DROPPED ON HER HANKY MADE OFLACE.

HER EYES MOVED QUICKLY TO THE DOOR
AS SHE HEARD THE KNOCK SHE'D HEARD BEFORE
SHE DARE NOT MOVE, SHE DARE NOT SPEAK
HER HEART BEAT FAST AND HER LEGS GREW WEAK.

THE DOOR SLOWLY OPENED AND A LIGHT SHE COULD SEE
A VOICE SAID IT'S ALRIGHT DARLING IT'S ONLY ME
FOR I'VE BEEN WAITING FOR A LONG LONG TIME
AND NOW I KNOW YOU'LL SOON BE MINE.

WITH OUTSTRETCHED ARMS SHE FOLLOWED HIM
INTO THE LIGHT HER DARLING JIM
GONE FROM THIS WORLD, BUT NOW HAPPY AND FREE
AND NOW TOGETHER THEY WILL ALWAYS BE.

SO

MY LOVE WEARS RIBBONS IN HER HAIR
SHE HAS NO TIME FOR TALKING
FOR TODAY SHE IS GOING TO BUY FOR ME
SOME SHOES TO GO A WALKING.

MY LOVE IS GENTLE LIKE THE DOVE
AS SHE LOVES ME SO COMPLETELY
FOR YESTERDAY I BOUGHT HER A GOWN
THAT FITTED HER SO NEATLY.

MY LOVE SAYS SHE WILL MARRY ME
WHEN WINTER TURNS TO SPRING
SO TOMORROW I WILL GO TO TOWN
TO BUY A WEDDINGRING.

REPENTANCE

I ONCE KNEW A MAN WHO HAD RICHES AND GOLD
HE HAD HOUSES AND LAND BUT AN EMPTY SOUL
FOR HE WENT AS HE SPENT NOT GIVING A CARE
FOR THE POOR AND THE NEEDY WHO HAD NOWHERE
HE GAMBLED AND DRANK TILL HIS MONEY RAN OUT
TO HELL WITH YOU ALL HE WOULD STAND UP AND SHOUT.

AS TIME SLOWLY PASSED HE FOUND OUT AT LAST
THAT HIS LIFE HERE ON EARTH HAD BEEN WASTED
HE HAD RICHES AND GOLD AND PLEASURES UNTOLD
BUT OF BEAUTY AND LOVE HE HAD NOT TASTED.

SO HE GATHERED TOGETHER HIS RICHES AND GOLD
AND HE SOLD ALL HIS JEWELS AND TREASURES
NOT MANY WERE LEFT AND HIS HEART GREW COLD
AS HE SAID GOODBYE TO HIS PLEASURES.

THEN HE LOOKED UP TO HEAVEN AND UTTERED A PRAYER
DEAR LORD UP ABOVE PLEASE SAVE ME
THEN TURNED HIS HEAD AS A GENTLE VOICE SAID
DEAR SON, I'M THE LORD YOUR SAVIOUR.

THESHIP

STANDING THERE IN ALL ITSGLORY
THAT WORN OUT SHIP COULD TELL MANY A STORY
FOR SHE SAILED THE OCEAN FAR AND WIDE
WITH THE LONELY SEA BIRD FOLLOWING BEHIND.

THE THUNDER AND LIGHTNING STRIKING THE DECK
TURNING HER INTO A SEA GOING WRECK
BUT HOMEWARD SHE'S HEADING AND HOMEWARD SHELL GO
COME HEAVEN OR HELL SHE WILL CONQUER THE FOE.

BATTLES SHE WON AND BATTLES TO HER COST
AND MANY A LIFE TO THE SEA SHE HAS LOST
LONG AND LONELY VOYAGES SHE HAS SAILED
AND REACHED HER DESTINATION NEVER FAILED.

BUT NOW HER SEAGOING DAYS ARE THROUGH
I KNOW COS I WAS ONCE ONE OF HER CREW
I'VE SEEN HER UP AND I'VE SEEN HERDOWN
NOW SHE'S HOME TO REST IN HER OWN HOMETOWN.

NOT IN VAIN

LITTLE CHILD SO DELICATE THERE
SITTING IN YOUR SMALL WHEELCHAIR
YOUR EYES SHINE BRIGHT AS PRECIOUS JEWELS
WHILE PEOPLE LOOK POINT AND STARE.

IT SEEMS SO SAD TO SUCH AS I
THAT CANNOT SEE THE REASON WHY
A LITTLE CHILD WHOS DONE NO WRONG
IS BORN TO LIVE, TO SUFFER THEN DIE.

AND YET I KNOW ITS NOT IN VAIN
THEIR LITTLE FACES SHOW NO PAIN
A HALO SHINES AROUND THEIR HEADS
A RAINBOW BRIGHT WHERE ONCE WAS RAIN.

SO WHEN THE TIME HAS COME TO GO
THEY LEAVE BEHIND A SPECIAL GLOW
AND SHINING IN THE SKY AT NIGHT
A STAR WILL TWINKLE SPARKLE BRIGHT.

THE GYPSY GIRL

AROUND THE FIRE LATE AT NIGHT
A GYPSY GIRL DANCED OH WHAT A SIGHT
THE MUSIC FILLED MY VERY SOUL
SITTING BY THE FIRE OFCOAL.

SHE CAME CLOSE TO THEFIRE
AND WHISPERED SHYLY I LOVE YOU
MEET ME LATER BUT NOT OUTDOOR
THEN MAYBE I'LL DANCE FOR YOU SOME MORE.

I WATCHED HER WHIRLING SKIRT GO BY
HER EYES THEY WERE A DANCING
SHE LOOKED AT ME THEN GAVE A SIGH
MY HEART WAS WILDLY PRANCING.

THE GYPSY VIOLINS WERE SWEET
THE AIR WAS FULL OF MAGIC
THE MUSIC HAD A SOULFUL BEAT
THAT TOLD OF LOVE S O TRAGIC.

SHE DANCED UNTIL THE MOON CAME OUT
ROUND AND ROUND THE FIRE
THEN WITH GAY ABANDON SHE DID SHOUT
COME KISS ME HANDSOME SIRE.

NOW IN THE FLICKERING FIRE LIGHT
I KNOW I'LL NEVERFORGET
THE VIOLINS AND THE GYPSY GIRL
AND THE NIGHT OUR TWO EYES MET.

Printed in Great Britain
by Amazon